David McCann is a film maker and producer of two short films set in 1920s Ireland titled *Sgt Collins RIC* & *The Green Fella*. He has worked as a hospital porter and an Irish Police Officer in the Garda Reserve. He lives in Enniskillen, Northern Ireland.

Books by David McCann

The Green Fella
A Boy Called Yank

David McCann
2/12/23

A BOY CALLED
YANK

DAVID MCCANN

FORESHORE PUBLISHING

Published in Great Britain in 2023 by
Foreshore Publishing Ltd
The Forge 397-411
Westferry Road, Isle of Dogs,
London, E14 3AE
Reg. No. 13358650
www.foreshorepublishing.com

The home of quality short fiction.

Set in Garamond Pro
Typeset by Deepak Gupta
Printed and bound in Great Britain by 4Edge Ltd, Essex.

ISBN 978-1-7393949-0-5

1

Connor Cleary peered out from the blankets of his comfortable, warm bed. He felt totally safe. Nobody could get him here, he thought. The bedroom was small and neat with bare walls, and a little brown dressing table in the corner of the room was his only luxury. Looking out of the window of his home at 1 Cleary's Cottage, Connor could see that it had snowed a little during the night. I'm not happy to see snow, he thought. Most 13-year-old boys would love to see it, but not me, and it is even worse when it melts – a horrible, slushy mess everywhere. I also know that today is a school morning and that is more bad news. Staying here in bed all day would make me the happiest boy in all of County Fermanagh. Connor pulled the blanket up over his head and sighed.

***

I pretended to be asleep when Kathleen came into the room but she was not going to fall for that old trick. She opened the curtains, pulled back my bedclothes and began to sing loudly. "There was a wild colonial boy. Connor Cleary was his name. He was born and bred in Ireland in a place called Castlecoole. He was his mother's only son, his father's pride and joy, but a terror to Australia the wild colonial boy." She shook the bed very hard. "Get up! Get up!" she cried.

"It's not fair!" I cried but I still had to get up.

I got up from my bed and washed my face with water from our white washing bowl, which helped to make me wide awake. I quickly put on my shirt, woollen jumper, short trousers, socks and boots. I stood up straight, tall and thin at our mirror, but I still could not make myself smile.

Kathleen is my mother. She called me into the main room of the cottage. The fire was burning and it warmed up the whole room; its orange glow lit up the few pictures on the wall. Number 1 Cleary's Cottage stands near the grounds of Castlecoole House, about six miles from the small market town of Enniskillen in County Fermanagh. Our cottage has whitewashed walls, a thatched roof and a red door. Inside the cottage we have one big room and two smaller rooms; one is my bedroom and the other is my mother's. The cottage was built by my great-great grandfather, Reginald, in 1843, exactly one hundred years ago.

Kathleen smiled her big smile at me. "Connor, sit down at the table and have your breakfast."

"Yes, Mother," I said sullenly and sat down to eat. Breakfast was always porridge with tea, bread and jam. "Mother, someday can we eat something else like bacon and eggs for a change?"

Just as I said that, old Ned Cleary came back from his morning dander. "Don't you know there is a war on, boy?" he said sharply. "The problem with children and young people today is you're all spoilt rotten." Old Ned leant on his walking stick as he shuffled up to the kitchen table, his favourite tobacco pipe in his other hand. He grinned slightly when he spoke to me again. "When I was your age I joined the Army and became a drummer boy. After a few years I became a soldier." He raised his walking stick and pointed to a picture of himself on the cottage wall.

I looked at the faded picture of my great uncle in his Army uniform. The picture was black and white but I know it was khaki with a pith helmet.

Old Ned spoke again. "I was 25 years old when that picture was taken. First battalion, Inniskilling Fusiliers, in South Africa during the Boer War. I will tell you about it someday."

"That is one thing you never talk about," said Mother.

Old Ned didn't answer her, he just glanced at his portrait and reminisced about old times. "You can't see it with my helmet on but I had a great head of brown hair. Now I have only a bald head, but I am 75 years old and the girls would not be bothered." He laughed and sat down at the table.

"Take that mug of tea," said my mother as she handed it to him.

I looked across the table at my two family members. "Life is so boring, Mammy," I said.

"Don't be silly, boy," said Old Ned. "As I said a minute ago, life is what you make it."

My mother spoke in a quiet but serious manner. "Connor, 13 is a strange and difficult age but you must get a job soon or find a hobby, something like football or boxing."

I didn't think long or hard about what she said. I had my answer ready. "The only thing I do is hit my Hurley ball with my hurling stick, from the front door of the cottage, through the bicycle tyre that hangs up on the rope tied to the big tree." I stopped for breath. "I don't like any other thing in this world like football, boxing, tennis. I don't know what I want to work at when I grow up and even today, it's snowing and it's cold. I hate snow. I hate everything."

Old Ned lost his temper with me a little. He stood up from the table and growled, "For God's sake, boy, it is December in the year of our lord 1943, winter time in Northern Ireland. It always snows at this time of the year. Live in the real world with the rest of us."

Old Ned got up from the table and went to sit by the big turf fire. Mother went over to the sink and washed the breakfast plates. I tied the laces on my ankle boots then got up, put on my warm brown duffel coat and walked to the front door. I know that it's December 1943 but I'm still not impressed and I don't really care. Life is still very boring.

Mother walked away from the sink and towards me. She was carrying my school satchel and a box with my gas mask in it.

"Mother, there is no need for my gas mask. The Germans never fly their planes this far north," I said.

"That is not true, Connor. A German plane could fly over Enniskillen any time, day or night."

Just to keep my mother happy, I put the box tied with string over my head and wore it around my back. My school satchel hung at my back between the shoulder blades. A kiss on the cheek ushered me through our cottage door and I was out in a big bad world, ready for school.

Once outside, my attention to detail noticed that the snow that looked deep from my window was not too bad after all. It was still very cold and I put the hood of my coat up, which kept my head and ears warm. With hands firmly in pockets I walked down the lane towards the main road. Castlecoole was in view. It couldn't be called a castle in the traditional sense. A huge white marble house with columns and pillars, it was built in the 17th century by wealthy landowners and stood in acres of woodland and farmland. Castlecoole soon disappeared behind me as I made my journey to school down the tree-lined lane towards the main Dublin road.

Reaching the road, I could first hear and then see an early-morning train. Grey smoke quickly puffed out from the funnel of a black and red engine. It chugged and hissed as it pulled brown carriages across the Weirs Bridge. The bridge was made of iron painted red which was held up by grey stone supports. They stood either side of the riverbank.

I turned to where I was going and my heart felt heavy. Enniskillen was ahead of me. I listened to the sound of my boots crunching the snow and walked to town. This small town was normally surrounded by green fields as far as the eye could see, but this morning white snow covered all that. I could see Belmore Street in front of me but the small matter of Jubilee Street was on my mind. Jubilee Street was named after Queen Victoria's golden jubilee of 1897. For the Orange Order, it is a staunchly Protestant street and only they can live there. It is a dangerous place for Catholics to pass. I was nearly lynched there by a mob last 12th of July. A policeman saved me from getting beaten up.

Jubilee Street now, in December, does not look like much. It is a very small and narrow cobbled street with red-brick houses facing each other, but in July, in the middle of the Protestant marching season, it is decked out with red, white and blue triangular bunting above the street. Union Jack flags, the red cross on a white flag and a great big red Hand of Ulster in the middle fly in triumph on every house. Paintings of King William of Orange on his white horse adorn the walls and pictures of the King and Queen of England peer from every window.

An orange arch stands at the front of the street – it says, 'Catholics beware. Don't cross into this territory.' Thankfully today all was peaceful so I hurried past towards my school. I passed a large field called the Fairgreen and Enniskillen Railway Station, into Belmore Street. The Boer War memorial loomed and the Great War monument too. Now I was struck by a greater fear than of what happened in Jubilee Street. My school was right in front of me. Not any school, but the Christian Brothers' school. The one thing that will terrify and put the fear of God into a Catholic schoolboy more than the Orange Order is the Christian Brothers. We only saw Orangemen in July and at least their hatred of Catholics meant they avoided any contact with papists, unless it was for a fight, but Christian Brothers had us from Monday to Friday nearly all day at school.

My knees started to wobble as I walked through the main gates. My stomach was turning. I trembled and shook all the way to my desk. Our classroom was very quiet; no child would dare make noise in Brother Liam's class. I sat at my little brown desk looking at the grey brick wall waiting for our teacher to arrive. I stared at a picture of Jesus and prayed he would save us from Brother Liam.

My thoughts were not of being bored but of being scared. From now until when I got home, my class and I would be at the mercy of these people, and for men of God they showed no mercy.

2

I ran down Belmore Street through the melting snow towards Castlecoole and our cottage.

"Yippee!" I shouted. School was over for another day and it was time to go home. Running past Celtic Park playing field I looked over to notice that a fence and some huts were being built by men in blue denim outfits, but it didn't hold my interest. I was just glad to be out of that jail and away from Brother Liam and my so-called school friends.

I made my way in through Castlecoole's main gates at the front of the estate near the railway bridge and line. As I ran breathlessly to my home, again I saw near to the main house of the castle, another set of huts being built. Planks of clean wood were being hammered and sawn by more blue-clad men with strange accents.

"Connor! Connor!" Mother had spotted me coming up the gravel path to our cottage. "Your dinner is ready!" she shouted, and waved her hand at me.

"Yes, Mother. I'm here and I'm hungry."

I reached the safety of my front door at last. I wasn't frightened anymore, just back to being bored again.

"I need to practice my hurling skills, Ma, before dinner." So I picked up my hurling stick and little rubber balls, and tried to put the ball through the tyre tied to the rope hanging on the tree. My puck was very good. I put every ball through the tyre – that's one thing I was good at. Pity I couldn't do everything else as well. "Mother, come and see! I'm the best hurler in Fermanagh."

My mother came to look. "Yes, Connor, well done. Now come and eat your dinner."

It was getting dark as I went into the cottage. Taking my coat off, I sat down to eat. Old Ned was at the table too.

"That's a great spread of food to eat, Kathleen. You have done well as always."

Rationing was in force all over the county but because we lived in the countryside, it didn't affect us at all. Ned had a vegetable patch at the back of the cottage and grew everything we needed. He also caught wood pigeon, rabbits, hares and the odd pheasant from the forest nearby. Lough Erne is full of fish. Pike, trout and salmon often ended up on our dinner table.

I greedily started eating the food. Rabbit pie, potatoes and carrots washed down with hot tea. We also had two chickens, and a cow near the cottage was our own milk supply, so really we were well off. I ate the lot and felt full but still bored.

"Connor, I have something to show you," said Ned.

We both went out the back of Cleary's Cottage to find an old bicycle propped up against the wall. It was all brown and covered in rust. "I found this today when I was fishing. I'm going to fix it up for you. It will give me something to do."

I looked at the bicycle. "It is going to take a lot of work, Ned," I said.

Ned nodded his head. "I have plenty of time on my hands. Come on, Connor, we will go back into the house. It is starting to snow again."

December darkness was descending and snow was again falling on rural Fermanagh. My hope was that even though I hated the stuff, it would snow hard enough to stop me going to school tomorrow. Ned and I both went back inside.

"Jingle bells, jingle bells, jingle all the way. Oh what fun it is to ride in a one-horse open sleigh." I smiled a little at my mother who was singing a Christmas song. She waved to me. "Connor, come and help me put up the Christmas tree and decorations."

"Yes, Mother. I will." The cottage had no electricity – it was heated by a turf fire and lit by candles and paraffin lamps. So first we had to put up the blackout curtains on the doors and windows so no German aeroplane pilot could spot us and get his position. Then my mother took the tree and stood it up to see how tall it was.

"I chopped that down today," said Ned. "It is just the right height too, Kathleen."

Once it was placed in the corner of the room, Mother enveloped brightly coloured paper around its green branches from top to bottom. "That looks nice," she said.

"Yes," said Ned, "it is starting to take shape now."

Some small candles and baubles were tied to the ends of the branches. Ned put little wooden figures of angels and animals on other branches. Our Christmas tree looked really good. I was slightly impressed but I wouldn't complain to Mother or Ned. I would keep my feelings to myself but it had cheered me up a little bit, because it reminded me of Christmas when I was a small child. It truly was a magical time then.

"Connor, go and get a chair at the table and you can put our star at the top of the tree."

I went and fetched the chair and my mother was holding the big gold paper star.

"You know that star represents the star of Bethlehem that the three wise men followed from the east, and it brought them to baby Jesus, Connor."

"I know that" I said. "The Christmas tree wouldn't be complete without that star."

The big Christmas tree stood proud in the corner of the cottage. The coloured paper was hung on the walls and across the ceiling too, for our small family Christmas had started.

Ned hung three big woollen stockings on the fireplace. "That's for Father Christmas to leave our presents in," said Ned, and he went and sat down by the roaring orange fire.

I went to the window to look at the snow, hoping it had turned to a blizzard. Deep white drifts blanketed and covered Fermanagh. Now that was one thing to cheer me up – no school tomorrow and no Brother Liam to teach us.

My room was in gloom and darkness as I clambered into a warm bed. Mother had used the hot iron on the sheets and this gave me instant warmth. "Goodnight, Mother. Nighty night, Old Ned."

Mother answered, "Goodnight, son," but Ned was asleep already.

As I lay in bed and stared up at darkened walls, my thoughts again returned to being a little sad. I got up in the morning, ate breakfast, went to school, came home, and I did the same thing all over again day after day after day. That was my life and that's it. I put my head down on the pillow and drifted off to sleep.

The next morning I was woken by the cold. A shiver rushed through my freezing body and I turned over in shock. My teeth chattered and rattled. My bedclothes were icy too. There was only one thing to do – put my clothes on. I dressed quickly under the blankets; it was even too cold to get out of bed to get dressed. Shirt, jumper, underpants, short trousers and even socks were hastily fumbled onto my cold, shivering body.

"Connor," said my mother, "come over and have your breakfast."

Old Ned and Mother were sitting at the table. I sat down beside them to eat. It was porridge as usual; the steam was rising from the hot, runny mixture but I was so glad to see something warm. I immediately started to eat it.

"You're not complaining about horrible porridge this morning, Connor," said Ned.

I didn't answer him, I just gulped the warmth from the food into my body. I reached over to the teapot and poured myself a big mug of the boiling liquid, put the mug to my lips and drank it. I was now for the first time this morning feeling warm again.

My mother looked across the table at me. "Connor, I am giving you the day off school today. The weather is too bad."

My face erupted in a big smile. "YES, Ma. That is great," I said.

"But you're going to do some chores for me about the cottage," said Mother.

I was so happy about not having to go to school and face Brother Liam and the other boys, I would have built another steel railway bridge exactly like the Weirs Bridge for my mother and old Ned single- handedly. I got up from the table and went straight to the turf fire burning in the hearth. A sunny, warm, orange glow filled the cottage with much-needed heat. I stood with my backside to the fire and looked out at snow-covered Fermanagh. Thanks be to God I'm indoors, I thought.

3

"Connor, I have given you the day off school and you are not going to sit about. I need you to do some chores for me." Mother handed me two empty steel buckets. "Go to the water pump and fill up the buckets with fresh water. We need to wash the cottage floor and fill the sink and our tin bath."

I took the buckets and went outside. It had stopped snowing and a big, cold, clear blue sky greeted me. It was sunny and cold but I had work to do. I trudged up the hill towards the water pump. It was hard to walk in the snow; my feet disappeared from my shins down into the deep white powder. When I finally got to the pump I was very tired but I still had to get the water out. I hope it hasn't frozen over. Luckily, it had not. Reaching up with my arms to the long red handle, I rocked it up and down and water flowed into my first bucket, and then I filled the second one and I was ready to go back home with my heavy load.

As I walked with the full buckets, my arms felt like they had been stretched to the ground. Oh, God, this is hard, I thought. I'm sinking into the snow even more. It's tough to do but at least I'm not at school. That thought cheered me up slightly.

"What kept you, Connor? I thought you had gone to Omagh or Belfast for that water," said Mother jokingly.

"That's not funny, Ma," I said as I made it to the cottage.

She laughed and helped me inside and poured the water into a big saucepan on the fire. "I'm going to boil it and use it to wash the inside of the cottage," she said. "Go out again and get me more water."

"Oh, Ma, that's not fair. I will be tired in no time," I said.

Mother clicked her fingers at me. "Go and get more water and don't be cheeky. I will tell you when I have enough."

Again and again I walked through deep snow to the big red pump. My feet were getting cold as I worked hard to keep my mother and Old Ned in water. We swept dust off the grey stone floor with a broom and brush, careful not to hit our Christmas tree. I was so busy I didn't have time to be unhappy.

Once it was swept, Mother mopped the floor with boiling water. The mop swirled around, licking it clean in big swipes, then the table and chairs were scrubbed down with cloths, and after that, the plates, knives, forks and spoons all got a good cleaning. It was boring work but we had to do it; my mother could never live in a dirty home. We might not have been rich with money but Mother always said that a clean cottage kills germs and even though we were poor, it didn't mean that we couldn't have pride in ourselves, and cleanliness is also next to godliness.

Old Ned put more turf on the fire. It was lovely to feel the heat from it circle around the room.

"Connor, take a seat by the fire and we will take a cup of tea," said Mother.

I was exhausted with all the work. My whole body ached. I sat and stared into the fire. If this is what real work is like I'm not going to be much good at it. It is still only morning and I feel like this. I will hardly last the whole day. Imagine having to do this every day, six days a week, I'd be useless at it, totally useless. I'm feeling down again. Is there anything that I can do right in this world? I will never be much use when I get older.

Ned noticed that I looked sad. "You're moping again, boy. You have got to be positive. When I was your age I was away seeing the world. I will tell you all about when you get older."

I had heard him say that before. He always said it. Someday I would get his stories from him but at the moment I wasn't interested. For me, the only world I knew was my little world. I get up, go to school and come home, that is all I do and that is the way I like it. Even though there is a war, it has nothing to do with me. It might as well be on the moon because it has no bearing on my private world whatsoever.

"Right, Connor my boy, it is time to get back to work," said Mother she handed me an axe. "Go down to the edge of the forest and chop some wood for the fire." She also handed me a brown sackcloth bag. "Connor, fill the bag with chopped firewood and bring it back up to the cottage. Empty the bag and then go back down and fill it again and again until I tell you to stop."

Oh dear. This is going to be yet more hard work, I thought, but it is better than school.

My path was covered with thick, deep snow. Walking in it was hard work in itself. The axe was heavy so I carried it with the blade over my shoulder like a rifle and I walked down the hill towards two fallen trees at the forest's edge. Chop, chop, was the sound my axe made as it crashed into the wood. It splintered all over the snow-covered ground and I swept it into the sack. I would try to run uphill to the cottage; it would keep me fit.

Old Ned met me at the front door. "I will soon have that bicycle fixed," he said.

"That's nice," I said sourly. "It will be March 1944 before I can cycle it if the snow stays like this."

Ned laughed at me. "Don't you worry about that for now, just keep bringing the chopped wood for our fire tonight." I scowled slightly into myself and trudged back downhill for more firewood.

Again and again I marched up and down the hill from our cottage to the forest and back for more. The light was fading and the afternoon darkness filling the sky. I was tired; this was hard work. The wood at the cottage was piled up high. My mother came to the door. "Good boy, Connor. You have worked very hard today. That load of wood proves that."

I smiled at her. "Ma, I feel like the grand old duke of York."

She laughed loudly and started singing, "Oh, the grand old duke of York, he had ten thousand men, he marched them to the top of the hill, and he marched them down again."

We both went inside, shut the door and put more logs and turf on the fire. Old Ned was sitting by the fire smoking his favourite pipe.

"I feel cold more than you two. It's my old bones – they are creaking with old age."

My mother and I closed the curtains and put up the blackout curtains too. I didn't see what good they would do. Any German pilot flying tonight would have no problem finding his way with all this snow about. I sat down at the table to eat my supper. The warm orange fire heated and brightened the room. Mother had made a big pot of Irish stew; it was hard to get some of the stew's contents with the war on but she always found some other foods to make it with. Tea, bread and butter were also served and everything on my plate was wolfed down very fast.

"Work makes you hungry," said Old Ned and he also ate fast. "I've been fixing that old bicycle all day – it will be as good as new soon," he said as he swallowed more of the stew.

"Yes, Ned. Thanks for everything. I am looking forward to cycling again."

"And you can use it to do chores and messages too. Isn't that right, Kathleen?"

My mother smiled at me. "Yes, Ned. I'm sure he will."

"I think I will go to bed now, everybody. I'm feeling really tired," I said.

"That's fine, Connor. You worked well today, you really did," said Mother.

"I agree. That was a tough job. You worked hard." Old Ned agreed too.

I felt pleased. For the first time in a long time I'd been praised for something. "Thanks for saying that." I kissed Mother on the cheek and went to my bed to lie down for the night. My room was dark as I took off my clothes and put on my nightshirt. Putting my head around the blackout curtains, I noticed the stars dancing in the sky. I don't like dark evenings; my gloom had returned again. When I got into bed my thoughts were of being sad.

I know Mother and Ned said I did a good job working today but they were just saying that to cheer me up. I'm useless and there is nothing I can do properly. My world is our cottage, to my school and home again, that's all there is to it. I feel awkward and gawky every day of my life. I have no friends at school but that doesn't bother me too much. The only thing I'm good at is hitting my Hurley ball through the tyre on the hilltop tree; at least I can say that.

We have no radio in our cottage and never see a newspaper so I don't know what happens in the outside world and to tell the truth, I don't care. We are even cut off from what happens in Enniskillen. The cottage has no electricity or running water. No postman ever calls with letters. You must be important to receive letters in the mail so that is me off the list, but again, I don't care. What you never have, you never miss. My thoughts soon start to wander. All the hard work that I did today, carrying buckets of water and chopping wood and then carrying the wood up and down all day. Soon I drift off into a deep sleep.

4

A few days later and the snow had all gone but my fear of school was still with me and again, I

must face my fear head on by having to go to school. After breakfast I went outside to hit the Hurley ball though the tyre in a bid to calm my nerves but it was no use. My hurling skills were, as always, very good, but I couldn't stop thinking of Brother Liam.

Waving at my mother and Old Ned in the cottage, my walk to school began. At least today was Friday. I would be free Saturday and Sunday. The green Fermanagh countryside sprawled in front of me as I wandered slowly towards the town. I am drawn to the little camp of huts with a barbwire fence protecting it. The blue-suited workmen with strange accents have gone. I wondered what it would be used for. The huts looked neat and tidy; shiny new metal roofs sparkled in the bright morning sunlight.

When I passed the bigger camp at Celtic Park on the Dublin road the same sight greeted me. "What is going on?" I said out loud. Most of the British soldiers were away abroad. Why would they need a camp for them here? I soon forgot about the camps when I walked up Belmore Street to see the red-brick building of the Brothers' School in the distance. Now my terror returned once more.

The classroom had four rows of brown wooden desks with the chairs built into them. They opened up at the front to reveal a compartment to keep your books, pencils, or even an apple if I was extra lucky to have one. Desks faced towards the blackboard in four neat rows. There was never a word out of turn; all boys sat in silence. We knew what would happen if we didn't stay quiet and it might happen anyway.

Brother Liam strode into the room. "Good morning, boys," he said with a menacing snarl.

"Good morning, Brother Liam," we all said meekly. He walked to the blackboard; his huge muscular frame powered to his desk. "Before we see who is present or absent this morning we must discuss HELL." He smashed his brown leather strap down on the desk with anger and much force. It made us all jump. My heart was pounding very fast; it sounded so loud I think the whole class could hear it. "Hell, boys. That is where you will all be going if you commit sins against the lord." Brother Liam frothed at the mouth. "Hell is eternal damnation to a big furnace of flames; flames that roast your soul, flames that never end. A boiling, seething, roasting heat of fire and brimstone consuming all you sinners forever."

We all sat shaking in our desks as Brother Liam ranted on and on.

"You must avoid sins of the flesh or the devil will take and destroy your mortal soul."

I didn't know what he meant about sins of the flesh but I knew I wouldn't commit any just in case.

He sat down behind his desk and opened his book. "Right, boys, I want to see who is attending class today." The rage was still in his voice. "Jimmy Rodgers."

Jimmy spoke softly. "Present." "Reginald Love."

"Present."

"Connor Cleary." "Present," I said.

He continued the name call until we had all been accounted for.

At break time Brother took us out to kick a football in the yard. He stood at the top of the yard and we all stood at the other end.

"Right, boys. I want you to catch the ball in your hands and kick it back to me." He looked awkward in his black robes as he kicked the heavy brown leather ball down the yard towards us boys. I caught the ball and booted it straight back to him. "Good catch, Cleary. Well done." This went on until Jimmy Rodgers tried to run with the ball on the ground. "Rodgers, what do you think you're doing? If I catch you or anyone else trying to play soccer you will get the strap. We are playing our own Irish game of Gaelic football, not that garrison game. See me inside after break." He took the football from Jimmy and kicked it high into the cold, sunny, blue sky.

A huge surge of relief took over me. School was over again until Monday. I walked out through the school gates and into Belmore Street. I had escaped again and the weekend was mine. Walking down the street I could hear a band playing music in the distance. That was unusual. What would a band be doing playing music on Friday afternoon in Enniskillen? Looking towards the railway station my attention was attracted to a military silver band on the platform. They were wearing khaki uniforms and playing marching tunes that I had never heard before. A large crowd was standing at the railway station. I asked one of the railway porters what was happening.

"Where have you been living? Don't you know that the Yanks are coming?"

"Yanks?" I said. "What are Yanks?"

The porter looked at me in astonishment. "Yanks are Americans. We are waiting for the 3:45 train from Belfast to Enniskillen. On board the train are American soldiers who are going to stay in Fermanagh. Those two camps at Celtic Park and Castlecoole are going to house them until they go to England." The porter was a bit ignorant towards me; he then carried on down the platform so I stood with the crowds to wait for the troop train to arrive.

An old lady with white hair spoke to me. "Those soldiers are from the Royal Ulster Rifles. My grandson plays the trumpet in the band," she said. I smiled at her but didn't answer. I was too busy looking down the platform to see if I could spot any American soldiers. I walked towards the ticket office to get a better view.

A train could be heard in the distance, clicking and clacking down the track as it got closer. I could see that it was a bright red engine with huge puffs of grey smoke belching from the funnel. It pulled into the station to loud cheers from everybody there. As the carriage door opened lots of smartly dressed American soldiers got out. They wore green uniforms of highest quality. "My god, I am really impressed with them." British or Irish Army uniforms look rough-ready and very slobbish, but these boys looked like rich people. I stood on the platform in a daze. If I could be anything in the world right now it would be one of these soldiers.

They marched smartly and in time out of Enniskillen Railway Station and onto the Dublin road. Music from the Ulster Rifles band filled the air. The Americans had rifles and a big heavy kit bag which they carried on their back. What a sight I have seen today. I felt special to have been in town to view it and I watched them march down the road towards Celtic Park in an orderly fashion. When they made it into camp I quickly ran home to tell my mother and Old Ned.

"Ma, Ned, you won't believe who is in town. Soldiers! American soldiers!" I was nearly out of breath with excitement as I ran through the cottage door.

Old Ned smiled at me. "Ah, it's a grand life being in the Army. You get to see the world."

"Yes but the world has come to me today," I said.

Mother was less excited. "All those men in one place can't be a good thing," she said and went back to washing clothes in the sink.

Old Ned patted me on my shoulder. "Connor, come with me. I have another surprise for you." We went outside. "There you are. I fixed it." Standing up against the cottage wall was the bicycle that he took out of the lough a few days earlier. It now was shiny and painted black. A small wicker basket hung on the front and a silver bell was attached to the handlebar. "Jump onto its saddle," he said.

"I will. I'm going to take a look at the soldiers in Celtic Park." I jumped on my bicycle and pedalled towards Enniskillen.

At Castlecoole Camp a soldier stood at the front gate with his rifle. Behind the barbwire I could see the soldiers making their beds in the huts and getting it ready for them to live in. I cycled down to the bigger camp and the same thing was happening there too. What an exciting day today is. I have had more fun today than I've had all year.

The darkness of a winter's evening was closing in so I rode my bicycle back to the cottage. What a day. What a brilliant day.

After supper I went to bed. I wasn't feeling too tired, I just wanted to lie in bed and think about what had gone on today. The time was 12 midnight; Mother and Old Ned were fast asleep. For the first time in my life a spirit of adventure took hold of me. I know what I'll do. I'll ride my bicycle into the edge of town and see what Friday night looks like in town. Trembling with fear and excitement, I slipped out of my window, climbed aboard my bicycle and I went very fast towards Enniskillen. Because the blackout was on I couldn't see too much so I strained my eyes into the distance in case I ran into something, or even worse, something ran into me. When I reached the Fairgreen at the bottom of Belmore Street I could hear shouting coming from Andy Mc Connell's public house. I crept up behind the big hedge to see what was going on. American soldiers were fighting each other in the public house. The blackout curtains had been ripped down from the front window and the darkened male silhouettes reflected onto the pub's gas-lit walls grappled and punched each other in a mad frenzy. As I watched the fight I could hear sounds of a siren getting closer. Two Army cars and a lorry arrived and soldiers with white markings on their helmets got out. They also carried long white sticks and they blew whistles as they entered the public house. Those white sticks were not just for show as they beat all the fighting soldiers over the head with them and threw them into the waiting lorry. Wow. It was a bit of a shock to see that happen. I want to go home now. I have seen enough for one night.

A few feet from me I could hear crying. It scared me a little bit. "I want to go home. I want to go home," the voice sobbed. I stared into the dark hedge an image of someone began to take shape as my eyes adjusted to the blackness. A man in uniform was hiding in the hedge.

"Hello," I said. "Who are you?"

The sobbing stopped and a voice spoke to me. "My name is Thomas Schulman, private first class, 8th Infantry Division, United States Army."

"Wow. You're a soldier," I said.

"Yes, and I don't like it here one bit. I want to go home," he said.

"Where is home?" I asked.

"My home is in Brooklyn, New York," he stated proudly. He walked towards me and I put my hand out; we shook hands. "I have got to get out of here, back to the camp. The MPs will be looking for anyone in that pub."

"What are MPs?" I said.

"Military Police. That was them in the Jeeps, with white helmets and white truncheons. Can you get me back to camp?"

"Yes, Thomas. Get on my bicycle and I will take you there." The soldier looked very young to be in the Army but I didn't say anything to him.

"Hey kid, I forgot to ask you your name," he said. "It's Connor. What camp are you staying in?"

"The smaller one," he replied.

We both got on the bicycle and I pedalled back to where home was for both of us. Thomas wanted me to drop him off at the edge of the camp so he could sneak past the sentry on guard at the gate so I did.

"Connor, thanks for your help. I want you to come down to our camp tomorrow afternoon and I will get you a pass and you can meet the rest of the boys."

My eyes lit up. "That would be great, Thomas. I will call down tomorrow. Thanks." We shook hands again and I cycled back to the cottage.

Nobody in the cottage had noticed me gone as I crept back in to my room. Putting on my pyjamas and getting back into bed, I couldn't stop thinking about the day I'd had. What a day, what a day. My excitement continued until I fell asleep.

5

"Connor, where are you going on a Saturday afternoon?" said Old Ned as he put another lump of turf on the fire.

"Ned, I am going down to the camp with the American soldiers to see what is happening."

Old Ned grinned. "That is what you should do, Connor. Join the Army or the Navy and see the world. This is a one-horse town and somebody shot the horse."

I didn't answer him, I just jumped on my bicycle and started towards the camp, hoping that Thomas would be there to greet me. At the camp entrance a soldier stopped me. I stood at the barrier and spoke to him. "Good afternoon, sir. Can I speak to Private First Class Thomas Schulman?"

The soldier was holding his gun; he pointed it to the ground. "You want to speak to Thomas Schulman? Hold on and I will get him for you." He went to his sentry box and picked up the telephone. I couldn't hear what he said but I could see him speaking to somebody. He came back out. "Thomas will be over from his hut in a few minutes to see you."

A young man in green uniform started walking towards me at the gate. He was tall, thin and had dark brown hair like mine. In fact we looked similar, like long-lost brothers. "Hi, Connor," he said. I was thrilled that he remembered me from the darkness of last night's blackout. "Come in and meet the boys. Leave the bicycle at the sentry's office – it will be safe there."

We both walked towards the hut. It was semi-circular corrugated iron with a door and two windows at the front. "Is it warm, Thomas?" I asked.

"Not really but it will have to do," he replied.

Once in the hut, the soldiers were all sat on their beds. Some were reading, others were writing letters to home. They all stopped and put their hands out. "Hi. Gee, it's strange to meet an Irish kid. How are you?"

I nodded my head. "It's very nice to meet you all. Where in America do you come from?"

"My name is Matthew Henry from Mason City, Iowa," said one.

"My name is David Anderson from Gettysburg, Pennsylvania," said the second.

"My name is John Miller from Pasadena, Texas."

"My name is Paul Johnston from Omaha, Nebraska."

It sounded like every part of America had a soldier here in Enniskillen. Places I had never heard of before.

Thomas sat down on his bed. "Connor, sit there at the edge of my bunk and we will talk."

I looked up at the pictures on Thomas and the rest of the guys' lockers. My face went into shock. "Who is that, Thomas?"

He started laughing loudly. "That is Rita Hayworth. She is my girl." The others laughed too.

"My god. She is the most beautiful woman I have ever seen and she is in her bra and knickers!" Thomas and the guys laughed even louder.

"Connor, I'm joking with you. Rita Hayworth is a big Hollywood movie star. She wouldn't be interested in a boy like me but she is my pin-up for the wall. My eyes were transfixed on her. Never in my life had a looked at a woman with nearly no clothes on. My heart pounded madly; my knees felt wobbly; I thought I would faint. "Connor, she is not the only pin-up girl here. Matthew has Betty Grable for his," said Thomas. Again I was drawn to a photo of a near- naked woman. I was never interested in girls before, but seeing those pictures had awakened something deep within my brain and loins. From that moment, in the space of three seconds, I matured five more years. Paul Johnston had a photo of Lana Turner. My eyes had gone into overload. So many beautiful American women in one afternoon. I think I'm in love.

"Thomas, do you have a girlfriend?" I asked.

"Yes, her name is Lola. She lives in Brooklyn, New York. I will marry her when I get back home. What about you, Connor? Do you have a girl?" asked Matthew.

"No, I don't have a girl," I answered, but seeing those photos made me want one. Of course those women were beautiful; I wouldn't find one to look like that in Enniskillen.

Thomas opened a box beside his bed. He handed me a bottle with dark black water inside. "Here, drink this and I'll tell you what it is." Paul took out a bottle opener and ripped the top off. Taking a big swig from the bottle, my tastebuds were attacked with an unbelievable sensation.

"FANTASTIC!" I drank and drank, lots more. "What is this, Thomas?"

He smiled. "Coca-Cola."

"Coca-Cola. I will love this taste forever," I said. John handed me something with the word HERSHEYS written in white letters on red wrapping paper. "This is a candy bar for you," he said.

"Thank you," I said, and took off the wrapper and ate it. Again, my tastebuds went crazy. I was used to just eating porridge at this time of the day. I hoped the Americans stayed for good. A candy bar was an American name for a bar of chocolate. It was the same thing, just a different name, that's all.

Matthew reached into his green kit bag beside his bed. "Here you are, kid. I have another thing for you," he said.

It was a green peaked cap. He took a big black pen and wrote on it – YANK! "That is your new name from now on."

I was speechless. A tear came to my eye. "Thank you," I muttered and put it on. It might just have been an old green baseball cap that the soldiers wore when they were working or taking it easy in their hut, but to me it was a great feeling to be accepted as one of the boys. Nobody in my home town bothered too much about me, but these guys came from thousands of miles away and we were friends straight away. "I agree. From now on I will be called Yank," I said proudly.

By now the bright afternoon sunshine had turned to twilight. It was getting colder too. "Thomas, I must go home now. It was nice meeting you all."

"Okay, Connor, I mean Yank. I will walk you to the gate."

"See you again, boys," I said as I walked to the door.

They all waved. "Goodbye, Yank!" they shouted. I smiled as I walked out of the door.

Thomas led me to my bicycle still standing at the sentry's box. My baseball cap was still on my head. I had no intention of taking it off. "Okay, Yank, I will see you tomorrow," he said.

"Yes, okay. See you, Thomas."

I cycled out of the gate and up the lane towards my home. My mother and Old Ned were in their usual places in the cottage. "Ma, Ned, I was with the American soldiers down the road. It was great. I drank Coca-Cola, ate chocolate bars, the lot." I ran into the kitchen, excited and talking very fast.

"Calm down, calm down," said Ned. I sat panting in the chair. "Good. I'm glad you had a great day."

"Yes, must go to bed, got to get up again tomorrow." I went to bed but couldn't sleep. My excitement kept me awake for a long time.

The next morning I sprang from bed very fast. I dressed quickly and went outside for my bicycle. It was Sunday so I must go into town for mass. I flew down the road and soon I was at St Michael's Catholic Church in Church Street. Instead of going straight into mass I waited outside. The sounds of marching feet could be heard coming through the centre of Enniskillen. I looked down towards Blakes of the Hollow public house and could see the soldiers parading to church. They were in two smart green lines on either side of the street and stretched as far as the town hall at the top the hill. Their uniforms must have been the finest of any Army in the world. I felt honoured and privileged to stand and watch them. The soldiers, who must have been Protestants, went to the right into St McCartan's Church of Ireland Cathedral, and the other line went into the Catholic church. I couldn't see my friend Thomas Schulman in either of the two lines of men so I went on inside to mass.

After mass I went down to the camp. Outside, Thomas was standing on sentry duty. "Thomas, I was looking for you earlier. I didn't see you at mass or the Protestant service either."

Thomas laughed very loudly. "You will never find me at either service, Yank."

I looked at him, puzzled. "And why not?" I asked. "Why not? Because I'm Jewish, that's why not."

I laughed too. "Jewish? I have heard of that, but I have never met anyone Jewish before." I paused.

"Mind you, I never get to meet Protestants either."

Thomas looked puzzled. "You're not bothered about me being Jewish?"

"No, Thomas. I don't have anything against anybody."

Thomas pointed to his watch. "Look, I will get off sentry duty in the afternoon. I will borrow the Jeep and we will go into town. Are you interested?"

I spoke up straight away. "Yes! I'd love to." "Alright, meet me at 1400 hours."

"What?" I said, not knowing what 1400 hours meant.

"Two o'clock your time," he said. "And we will go for a drive in the Jeep."

"That's good. I will see you at two." Off I went back home to tell my mother who said the mass and who the priest was. It was proof that I had been to mass. My mother would find out all that information from another Sunday mass-goer and I'd be in big trouble if I didn't know all details.

Two clock came and I went down to meet Thomas. He was parked outside the barbed wire in his Jeep. It was a green car with no roof, just a window at the front so the driver is protected from the wind. A big white star was painted on the front bonnet and 'USA' was also written in white on a side panel at the rear.

"Thomas, how did you manage to get this?" I asked.

"I told the sergeant about our friendship and he wanted us to make more friends in the town. Said it would be good for Anglo-American relations."

Getting into the Jeep was very exciting. I had never been in a motor car and there I was, about to drive through town in a vehicle that nobody would believe existed. The engine purred and we drove off towards Enniskillen. Our Jeep took us down the Dublin road, past Celtic Park American Army Camp, into Belmore Street and onto the east bridge, over Bridge Street, up Town Hall Street and at the top of the town high street no other cars were on the road except us. I felt ten feet tall to be driving around town with my new friend.

Thomas paused the Jeep to look at a shop. "That's a pretty store," he said. I also stared at it.

"Yes, that's Trimble's Drapery – a family-run shop."

"My, it's pretty," said Thomas again.

We continued on down the high street towards the Hollow. Thomas slowed down to look at a public house. "That bar looks great."

"Yes, that's Blakes of the Hollow. That pub has been there since about 1890, I think."

Blakes had distinctive red and black stripes at the pub doors that made it stand out from the rest of the shops in the street. Driving up from the Hollow we passed the two churches – St Michael's Catholic Church and the Church of Ireland Parish Church with its tall spire. Thomas and I drove along Darling Street and then down into Anne Street and over the west bridge. When we got to the brook, Lough Erne could be viewed on our right-hand side.

Every curtain in the little houses twitched with vigour as the US Army Jeep passed by. It was such a privilege to drive through my town in this way.

We then drove along Willoughby Place and decide to visit Portora Royal School at the top of the hill. There was a good view of the town from up there. The Jeep soon reached the top of Portora Hill. "This a very famous school, Thomas. Oscar Wilde, a famous writer, went to school here," I said. He stopped and parked the Jeep. Towards the town we could see hundreds of chimneys pouring smoke up against the cold blue sky. We watched and imagined all Enniskillen people huddled around their fires, trying to keep warm on this cold December Sunday in 1943.

"Thomas, I want you to tell me how you got here and what home is like. I will sit quiet and let you speak."

Thomas spoke. "Alright. My name is Thomas Schulman, private first class, 8th infantry Division, United States Army, from Brooklyn, New York. I live with my father, mother, three brothers and three sisters. We are a big Jewish family. I also like sports. Baseball is my favourite and the Brooklyn Dodgers are my team. They wear blue and white uniforms and play their games at Ebbets Field." He paused to catch his breath. "The manager's name is Leo Durocher and my favourite players are Dolf Camilli, Joe Medwick, Whit Wyatt and Mickey Owen."

I looked puzzled. I had never heard of those men in my life before but it must have been the world to Thomas because his eyes lit up when he said all their names.

Pulling out two bottles of Coca-Cola, Thomas handed me one. "Here, have a drink. I'm thirsty." I was thirsty too, especially when this lovely dark, sweet drink was about. Thomas looked at me. "Tell me about your life, Yank."

I coughed. "My name is Connor Cleary. I'm an Irish Catholic, although that is not important. I live with my mother and Old Ned in Cleary's Cottage in County Fermanagh, and that is about it." It wasn't much to talk about so I changed the subject quickly. "Can this Jeep drive off-road on grass?" I asked.

"Of course," said Thomas. "I will show you." We roared downhill to the water's edge. "Come on. Get out of the Jeep and we will walk on the bank."

We both got out and I pointed across the water. "Those fields over there are called Cornagrade. Nothing but green fields. All the people from the Famine are buried there."

"What is the famine?" asked Thomas.

"The potatoes failed and Britain let the people starve to death so they buried them there."

Thomas didn't ask the question again. He must have felt uneasy about the subject. "Look," he said. "Stones. Watch me skim this one." He spun the stone and it bounced across the water four times.

"Watch me this time," I said. My stone bounced one, two, three, four, five times across Lough Erne. I picked up a shiny pebble at the side of the bank. "Here is a souvenir of Fermanagh, Ireland, for you to keep." I handed Thomas the pebble and he took it from me.

"Thanks. I will keep it with me wherever I go in this world." He put it in his pocket then bent down and reached for another pebble. "This is my sign of friendship to you. I want you to keep this with you always."

I took it in my hand, said, "Thank you, I will," and put the pebble he gave me into my pocket.

We then jumped back into the Jeep and drove very fast back up the hill to Portora School. We parked again, looking down on Enniskillen. I asked Thomas about the Army. "How did you join?"

"I joined the Army when I turned seventeen but I gave my age as twenty-one. That was in March of this year, 1943. My anger was still there from December 7th, 1941, when Japan bombed Pearl Harbor in Hawaii. They were Nazi Germany's allies so America must fight both of them, and the Nazis are persecuting Jews in Europe. So my father said that I must join the Army and put a stop to Adolf Hitler and his murderous gang."

Connor nodded his head. "Hitler is a madman. That is what Old Ned said to me."

Thomas spoke again. "I must say it has been tough coming to Europe and leaving my wonderful family but if this is what I have to do, I must do it." He sat and thought about home. "When I joined the United States Army we stayed at Camp Kilmer, New Jersey, then it was on to New York Harbor and a troop ship across the Atlantic Ocean to Belfast. I wouldn't make a good sailor; I was seasick all the way from New York to Belfast."

Connor looked across to town. Twilight was fast approaching. "Thomas, do you want to come to my cottage for tea?"

"Yes, that would be fine. I'd like that, Yank," he said jokingly.

The little Jeep set off down to Willoughby Place and back into town. It was in Willoughby Place that for the first time I spotted a girl. She wore a bright blue coat, and had long brown hair tied back behind her head. My stomach felt funny and my heart raced; it was the same feeling that I'd had when I saw Rita Hayworth on the hut wall. As we passed by I couldn't stop looking at her. She was the most beautiful woman in the world. I didn't say anything to Thomas. I was a bit embarrassed. She went in through the door of number 45 Willoughby Place. I must keep an eye out for her again, I thought.

When we went back through the town the second time, lots of people came out to see us. Old men, women and little boys and girls stood waving their arms at us. We both waved back. "My, everybody is so friendly here," said Thomas.

"Yes," I said. "They all seem glad to see us."

We took a few detours on our way back to camp, driving through Wellington Place then up Queen Street, Strand Street, Head Street, Mary Street, Abbey Street, and we stopped in Dame Street. "This part of town's nickname is the Dardanelles. It got that name because most of the men in these streets went out to Gallipoli in the First World War with the British Army. Most never came back – they were killed out there."

Thomas sat and thought deeply about that situation. "That is not a nice thought," he said.

I didn't answer him. I think it was too close for comfort; the similar situation he was in now, to those men in 1915, wasn't lost on him.

We soon reached my cottage. Mother and Old Ned came out to look at the strange car that we had arrived in. "Welcome to our home," she said.

"Why thanks, ma'am," he replied.

Old Ned walked over with his hand outstretched. "Hello, sir. Nice to meet you but your uniform is very smart. I hope you are not an officer. I'm an old soldier and I never liked officers too much."

Thomas roared with laughter. "Well, buddy, that makes two of us. I don't like officers much either."

Old Ned laughed too. There was a common soldiering bond between them straight away. We all went inside the cottage and Mother made tea and scones for everyone to eat.

6

Tea and scones filled our kitchen table. We all sat down to eat and talk.

"I would like to thank everybody for their warm hospitality today. You all couldn't have been nicer to me," said Thomas.

"The pleasure's all mine," said Mother.

"Yank, I mean Connor, told me that you were in the Army, sir."

Mother chuckled and interrupted. "Did you call Connor 'Yank'? Is that his new nickname?"

"Yes. That is what the guys in camp called him."

Old Ned coughed. "We will talk about his nickname later. Yes, Thomas, I was a soldier a long time ago – 1900 was the year."

"Did you see action, sir?" asked Thomas.

"Yes, in the Boer War. The event is burned into my mind – 24th of January 1900, on a hill called Spion Kop, which is near the Tugela River in Northern Natal, South Africa."

We all sat and listened to his story. Thomas didn't speak a word. It was as if he wanted some advice for his own battles yet to come.

"A shallow trench was dug at the top of the hill in which the British soldiers were positioned. The Boers attacked it with rifle fire and artillery; it was slaughter. The trench was called the murderous acre – 243 soldiers were killed there. The rest of the casualties numbered 1,500. It was the officers' stupidity that caused most of deaths. That is why I asked you, Thomas, if you were an officer. I don't like officers for that reason."

Thomas agreed. "I see your reason, sir," he said.

"My advice to you in battle, is don't be a hero. Keep your head down and you will get through. The job is just to survive."

Thomas was a little pale with all this war talk.

"Now, now, Ned. That's enough of that for today. I'll bet your mother and father are lovely people," said Mother, changing the subject.

"Yes they are. I miss them a lot."

Ned got up from the table and went over to a cupboard. He took out a bottle of clear liquid he handed it to Thomas. "There you go, boy. Bring that back to your men at the camp and tell them it is a present from Ned."

Thomas looked at the bottle. "What is it, sir?"

Ned laughed. "That is the best poteen from the Boho mountains of Fermanagh. It is the best distilled water in all of Ireland's 32 counties."

Thomas got up from the table. "Thank you all for everything. I must go back to camp. I will bring my own presents to you the next time I visit. You folks have been marvellous." He walked out of the door and got into the Jeep. "Connor, I mean Yank, you can come back with me. You have a pass and can visit anytime." I was delighted to accept and climbed into the Jeep with him and we roared off towards the 8th Infantry Division's new home for now.

At camp we pulled in past the gate and I could hear sounds of strange yet fantastic music coming from one of the huts. "Thomas, what is that?" I asked.

"American Patrol," said Thomas. "What is that, Thomas?"

Thomas looked at me. "American Patrol is a big band tune by Glen Miller. He is very famous in the States."

Glen Miller. I didn't know who he was but the music made me giddy with excitement. "Let's go in and listen to this music. It is amazing."

We rushed into the hut and the guys were all there.

"Hello, Yank. Where is your hat we gave you?" they all said together.

"It's in my pocket. I will put it on." Reaching into my pocket, I felt the pebble that Thomas had handed to me at the lough shore, then I pulled out my hat and put it on my head. "I promise to keep it on at all times," I said.

"Hey Yank, can you help us? We need some food and our clothes washed."

I scratched my head through my hat. "I will get my bicycle and take the clothes up to my mother. What kind of food would you eat? Tell you what, I will get fish and chips from the shop in town. I hope it's open on Sunday."

"Aww shucks, Yank, that will be great," they said. "But can I listen to Glen Miller first?"

"Of course you can," said Matthew. "Here, have some more Coca-Cola and candy bars."

"Yes please," was my happy reply. This is truly amazing. I'm sitting here, listening to Glen Miller, drinking sweet Coca-Cola. It's a beautiful world. Before Friday my life was boring and now look what has happened. The world has come to me in wonderful colour. It's like I am sitting on a rainbow. I don't want this day to end. The music is like nothing I have ever heard before or will again. I'm drunk with happiness. I have done more things in two days than I have ever done in ten years. Long may it continue.

I watch Thomas take the pebble from his pocket and put it in the footlocker under his bed. "This Irish pebble is coming with me to France, Germany, or wherever the 8th Infantry Division travel to in Europe to fight the war. Thanks, Connor. You are a true friend."

"Alright, boys, get me your clothes to wash ready. My bicycle is at home. I will go and get it and come back down."

As I went to the door, Thomas pulled out the bottle of poteen. "Look, boys, genuine Irish moonshine," he said they all cheered and clapped. "You can thank this boy Yank and his old soldier relative for this present."

"It's no bother, lads. Anytime." I ran back home for my transport. I now had work to do.

I went back to the camp and all the soldiers gave me money to get them their fish and chips. It was beautiful to see all those pounds, shillings and pence in my hands. I beamed and my eyes lit up. "Thomas, I have never had so much money. In one day, I'm rich. Wonderfully rich."

He smiled. "Okay, now go and get your job done."

On my ride home all the soldiers' clothes poured out of the basket at the front of my bicycle. I had a job to keep it from falling onto the dirty ground. "Ma, Ma? Can you take these clothes to wash?" I shouted as I reached home. "I need to go to town and find a chip shop that is open on a Sunday."

Mother gathered the heavy bundle in her arms. "Oh, give here," she said. "What do you want, to make work for me?"

I ran to my room and put some of the money into my sock drawer. The troops had given me too much because they are just used to dollars and whatever their coins are, and my shiny pebble that Thomas had given me earlier at the lough shore was placed carefully into my drawer. "Don't worry, Ma, you'll get paid for doing it. I'm a rich boy."

Wind rushed around my green baseball cap. 'Yank' was proudly written on it in black ink. I pedalled swiftly towards Enniskillen in excitement, hoping that food was available for the boys. Very soon I spotted one open. Gordon's of Water Street always served food on Sunday. I left the bicycle outside and walked into the shop. A warm, hungry smell of hot oil filled my nostrils.

"I don't think you can afford chips here," said the man behind the big glass counter. He stared at my cap. "Yank," he laughed. "Yank?"

I took a big ball of money out of my pocket. "Give me ten fish and chip suppers, please."

His chin almost hit the floor in shock. "Where did you get that money, Yank? Did you steal it?"

I tapped his counter with a two-shilling coin. "No, I did not, this is for the American soldiers down in the huts at Castlecoole."

He looked again at the cap I was wearing. "And that's where you got that hat."

Taking out a pound note, my hand waved at him. "Don't worry about money. Please just get me ten fish suppers."

He stopped grinning. "Listen to me, Yank boy.

Don't be cheeky or you will get nothing at all."

I put my head down. "Okay. Sorry, sir. Can I just have the food?"

He started cooking and did not talk to me again, and when it was cooked he wrapped it in old newspapers and handed them to me. Carefully I put my hot, tasty feast into the basket and rode back for camp.

As I walked into the hut the sound of an extraordinary voice stopped me dead in my tracks. I listened intensively, mesmerised as this wonderful sound washed over me. My very soul shook with wonderment. Thomas had noticed the look on my face. "That singer is a man called Frank Sinatra. He is a big star back home in the States. He always sings about being in love."

When I heard that song I couldn't help but think about that nice-looking girl I saw in the blue coat today. "Frank Sinatra. I think I'm going to be a big fan of his from now until I die," I said. "Here is your fish and chips."

Thomas took the tightly wrapped bundle of newspaper from me and put it down on the table next to the window. "Okay, men, it's chow time." They all started eating what I had brought them.

"Hey, this stuff is good, Yank," said Matthew. Everybody else grunted in appreciation and continued to eat.

Thomas winked at me. "Keep the change," he said. "Okay," I answered in return.

After the meal I had to go home. Thomas walked me to the gate.

"What is it like to be a Catholic?" he asked.

"I don't feel any different to anybody else," I said. "And what is it like to be Jewish, Thomas?"

"Oh, just the same as you. After all, we are just human beings. We might look different on the outside but our souls inside are the real me and you."

"Yes and you, Thomas, have the same colour of skin as me, so there is no difference and we both look the same. Jewish people are white too."

Thomas nodded his head and agreed. "Where I live in Brooklyn, Jewish people and Italians don't get along together. They call us Christ killers and other nasty things."

I took this to heart. "That is silly, Thomas. How could Jewish people be called Christ killers? In the bible it was the Romans who killed him by crucifixion" Thomas laughed loudly "yes you are right Connor it was the Romans who killed him."

"When I write to my father I will tell him to say that to anybody who says that."

I thought about it again. "And you can also tell him, if an Italian says that Jews are Christ killers, that in fact it was them who killed him because Romans are their ancestors."

Thomas patted me on the back. "That is very funny and true. In fact, I will write to him tonight and tell him what you said, just in case I forget."

We both walked towards the main gate. My bicycle clanked and clicked as I pushed it forward.

"Connor, I will see you tomorrow. I don't know what time because us GIs are going to somewhere called Florence Court to the shooting range."

"I will see you tomorrow, Thomas." We said goodbye and I cycled up home with the magic of Glen Miller and Frank Sinatra ringing in my head. We must get a wireless radio now. We must. Look at all the great things and sounds we are missing, I thought. The whole world is out there and is passing us by. Mother and Old Ned must get one for Christmas. That is a good excuse, if any.

7

School was over again for another day and I walked home filled with relief. Brother Liam was his usual sadistic, bad-tempered self. Our whole class got strapped with two of the best from him. I can't wait to leave school. I don't know what work I want to do but I would break rocks with my bare hands just to be out of that terrible dump.

When I reached the cottage my first thought was to go and see Thomas. "See you all later. Must dash to Thomas. Bye for now. Ma, please can we get a wireless? We are missing the whole outside world without it. There is more to our lives than what happens in this town."

She looked a bit shocked that I was leaving so soon but nodded her head in agreement. "I have wanted a wireless so long. I think it is time we had one," she said.

"Thomas is waiting. I will talk later," I muttered and went outside and started walking to the camp. My green 'Yank' cap was taken from my pocket and I put it on my head.

On reaching the gate a sentry waved me through. "Come on in, Yank," he said.

I felt very proud and honoured to be let in. Not everybody got this treatment. My heart was almost bursting from my chest with pride.

"Hi there, Yank. Good to see you," said Thomas.

My face lit up with delight. "Hi to you too," I replied. "What have you done today?"

Thomas handed me a bottle of Coke. "We have been out on the shooting range this morning with our rifles. It's tough to wake at five in the morning."

"I was at school today but I'm going to leave soon and get a job. I don't know what work to do."

Thomas sat on his bed and went back to cleaning his rifle.

"What sort of gun is that?" I asked

"That, Connor, is an M1 Garand rifle. Standard issue for a GI and a deadly killing machine in all weathers, hot or cold. Every GI gives their weapon a girl's name. Mine is called Lola after my girl back home in the States." Thomas stopped cleaning his rifle and stared at the floor. He was deep in thought. "Lola. I'm going to marry that beautiful girl when this war is over. I love her and I miss her."

I spoke softly. "Thomas, how do you know when you're in love with a girl?"

He looked at me. "Well, you get a sickly feeling in your stomach every time you see her, and your knees tremble."

"I saw a girl when we were out in the Jeep and I got that feeling. She was wearing a blue coat and I think of her a lot."

Thomas smiled. "That's an infatuation, it's not love. She has to feel the same way about you, then it's love." Thomas scratched his head. "Say, why don't we find out who this girl is and you can ask her out on a date?"

"A DATE? No, I couldn't. I would be too scared. I have never really talked to a girl before, never mind asking her out."

"We will soon sort that problem out. Let's go into town later and see if we can spot her."

I shook with fear at the thought of asking her out and drank almost all the cola in one big gulp.

We both walked into town. Thomas had a pass from camp that only lasted two hours. "You must tell me what this girl looks like," he said.

"No problem, but you must not go over and tell her. Let me do that in my own time." "Agreed," he said.

It was getting dark and the streets had a few shoppers milling about. A black motor car drove by slowly, honking its horn at a small dog that had walked in front of it, and then I saw her. "Thomas, that's her."

He stared over at the girl in the blue coat. "My, she is pretty. I can see why you like her."

We watched her as she went into Trimble's drapery shop in the high street and Thomas and I followed her inside. It soon became clear that this was the family-run business. "Listen for her name being called," said Thomas. "I will go up to the counter and speak to the man there." He went towards the assistant and smiled. "Good evening, sir. My name is Thomas Schulman from Brooklyn, New York, and this is a mighty fine store you have."

"Thank you for the compliment. My name is Gordon Trimble and this is my shop." Then the girl I liked came around the counter she had taken off her blue coat. "And this is my daughter, Jill. She works here every day after school."

Thomas turned on the charm. "Why it's very nice to meet you, Jill. You are very pretty."

She stood and blushed. "Thank you," she said.

"Well it's been nice talking to you folks but I have got to get back to the rest of the soldiers." Thomas coolly bid Jill and her father Gordon goodbye and the two of us went back outside onto the high street. "There you are, Connor. The ice is broken. Now you know her name and where she works, and you also know where she lives."

I looked at him as we walked towards Town Hall Street. "Yes, Thomas, and I wished that I didn't know because I can't go on a date with her."

Thomas looked puzzled. "Explain to me why," he said.

"Why! Because she is a Protestant," I answered.

Thomas stopped dead in his tracks and gripped my sleeve. "I thought you said that you have no prejudices."

"No, I don't. I would love to ask her out on a date but her family wouldn't let it happen. Her father was nice to you but he would be one of those staunch Unionist Protestant shopkeepers that would never have a Catholic about the place, so I have no chance of going out with Jill. That is reality of living in Northern Ireland in 1943."

Thomas was taken aback. "Sorry, Connor. I didn't think things were like that but I think that is so stupid. I mean, you're Catholic and I am Jewish and we both get along fine. It's like everything else in life – we will have to overcome this too. After all, we are just human beings."

"You are so right but also my confidence with girls is very bad. In fact, they frighten me."

Thomas tutted. "Frightened of girls. That is also stupid. We will soon stop that. Girls are human beings too. They are not from Planet Mars or anything. I will help you there too. Now you must ask Jill out on a date soon."

"Yes, I agree. Hopefully my chance is yet to come but I need your help."

As we walked to camp I thought about what he said. It is stupid that religion or politics can come between taking a girl out. "Thomas, I have thought of another problem. She doesn't know I fancy her."

"Don't worry. She will soon get to know you – that is our next task."

As we both walked up the Dublin road my thoughts were filled with how to ask Jill for a date. I would have to try and meet her on her walk home from the shop.

At camp we both said goodbye and agreed to meet tomorrow, and I thought about Jill as I made my way home.

8

Brother Liam had us boys back in the school yard. "Right, you lads, I want you all facing me
and I'm going to kick the football up into the air and you must catch it and kick it back to me," he bellowed in his menacing voice. We all did as we were told except one boy who wanted to dribble the ball, soccer style. "Rodgers, see me in class, boy. I'll put this idea of garrison games out of you once and for all." We all trembled. Brother Liam was in a very bad mood. We all were going to get it in the classroom.

"Right, Rodgers, come to the front of my class now." Everybody took their seats except for Jimmy Rodgers. As he reached the front Brother Liam grabbed him by his jumper and slapped his face. "You cheeky, impudent little sod. Don't defy me anymore, boy." Jimmy was then thrown against the desk and belted around the backside. He was lifted up by his ears and slapped once more across his face. Brother Liam's face was purple with rage. "Alright,

Rodgers, you will never play soccer again in my yard. Now hold out your hand." Jimmy stood with his arms stretched in front of him. The strap was brought down on his pale white hands with much force and venom. One, two, three, four, five and six of the best. We all sat like little mice and never spoke a word just in case it could be our turn to face the wrath of Brother Liam.

"Now boys, I'll show you all just who runs this place. Everybody stand up and make a line walking to my desk." We all did what we were told like frightened little sheep. "Alright, put your hands out as you walk by me." Again, we did as we were told and he strapped us on each hand. I went back to my desk with my hands numb and burning. I folded them over my chest to stop the pain. Tears rolled from my eyes and onto my cheeks but I wiped them off with my sleeve just in case Brother Liam saw me cry and strapped me again for being a big baby.

When class was over for the day my thoughts were focused only on meeting Thomas for another talk. I had learned more from him than any teacher in this world could show me and I walked to the camp once more. The sentry waved me in. "Yank," he called. "You have a special pass anytime to come in." Again, that made me smile.

Thomas sat on his bunk. He looked tired. "How was your day?" he asked me.

"Terrible," I answered. "We got beaten and strapped by Brother Liam."

Thomas looked puzzled. "I thought he was a religious man."

"That is what I thought too but he has lots of power and he uses it," I said.

"Our Rabbi would never be allowed to get away with that. He would be put in jail," said Thomas.

"I should become Jewish instead of a Catholic."

Thomas smiled. "You always make me laugh with your wonderful innocence. I agree, you should be Jewish like me." We both laughed at the thought. "Connor, I need to get some sleep. Why don't you come back at seven o'clock tonight? We are going to watch two movies in the big tent."

"What is a movie?" I asked.

Thomas looked at me. "It's a moving picture show."

I knew then what he was talking about. "In Ireland we call that a film. What are they about?" I said.

"They are both comedies. Laurel and Hardy and A Night at the Opera by the Marx Brothers," said Thomas.

"Yes, okay, I'll come down then. But after the day I've had I could do with not seeing any more 'brothers' in my lifetime." We both said goodbye and I made my way home to see Mother and Old Ned.

"Hello, stranger," said Old Ned. "Since the American Army came to stay in town we have not seen you very much. To tell you the truth I'm glad for you because you have now got a life. Before they came you just moped about the cottage all day," he said sharply.

Then Mother spoke. "You have changed for the better, Connor. You have become a little bit more grown-up. The next thing I want you to think about is leaving school and getting a job."

"I want to leave badly, Ma, but I haven't thought about what I want to do. Talk to you later about it. I'm going for a lie down. I'll be up for seven o'clock. We're watching a film in the big tent at the camp." With those words I went to my room and lay down.

When I arrived back at camp Thomas and the other soldiers were already in the big tent. I was ushered in and sat down next to Matthew and Thomas. "Sit down next to us, Yank," said Matthew.

"No problem," I said.

The tent was dark and filled with cigar smoke. Our only brightness came from the film machine which shone onto the big white screen in front of us. We all sat, hushed, not making a sound. I had never been to the pictures before in my life so I had been looking forward to this night. Laurel and Hardy, one thin man and one fat man, both in bowler hats, appeared on screen. We all screeched with laugher with all the mad, stupid things they did to each other. When I thought of bowler hats Orangemen marching came to mind but this was the first time ever that hadn't happened. From now on it would be Laurel and Hardy.

After that, the next film to come on starred the Marx Brothers. Groucho was my favourite, with his cigar, glasses, grease paint moustache and smart wisecracks. I wanted to be like him in town tomorrow. We all roared with laughter. My sides were sore from laughing. This is so funny.

When the picture show was over I said goodbye to Thomas and went home. It was now a dark, clear night; the stars danced and sparkled in the sky. It was very cold and because it was nearly Christmas all I could think of was the three wise men crossing the cold desert on camels to bring gifts to Mary, Joseph and baby Jesus in the stable in Bethlehem. I could almost see their shapes pass by me on this freezing Fermanagh hillside. Reaching the safety of my cottage, my ears could hear music. It can't be. Mother must have got us a wireless. I opened the door and sure enough, there on our table was a big brown box with black dials, lit up in the middle. "Hello, Ma and Ned. It's great to see that wireless."

Mother got up from her chair by the fire and put some more turf on to burn. "This is the life. It is good to be here now. What more could a person want? Sitting by the fire, listening to our new wireless," she said. For once I had to agree with her. There was no place in this world that could match the feeling of sitting there in our cosy cottage. I felt safe, warm and protected. It was hard to believe that World War Two was raging its murderous destruction across Europe and the Pacific with a violent orgy.

Old Ned nodded at Mother. "You are so right, Kathleen. Think of the sailors out on Atlantic convoy duty tonight, in harm's way on the big, cold ocean." He blew smoke from his pipe and settled back in his chair, deep in thought.

We all listened to the Christmas carols that were coming from the wireless. "We three kings from orient are," sang the choir. I looked out the window and again I could imagine the three wise men on their camels crossing the hillside on the way to Bethlehem.

9

June 1944 arrived very quickly. Seven months went by in the blink of an eye. The day was hot and sunny and I still had not got around to asking Jill out on a date, but I decided that today was the day to do it. My stomach churned with fear. I had never asked a girl out before; this was a new experience for me. "Courage is what is needed but does she like me?" I said to myself out loud. Jill's grand Georgian house looked towards Lough Erne and over to the shore at Cornagrade. My hiding place was behind the grey stone wall that straddled the full length of the brook terrace and road.

My heart was pounding with fear as I scanned the road hoping to catch a glimpse of my most favourite girl in the world. Rita Hayworth wouldn't hold a candle to Jill; she was beautiful beyond words. That's what I thought anyway.

Jill suddenly came into view at the top of the road and my poor little heart rushed madly. "Oh my god, there she is!" I shrieked. "What will I do? What will I say?"

She was wearing a long cream dress. Heaven was the only word I could use to describe what I was seeing before me. As I pulled myself up to get a better look my foot slipped on some wet grass. "Ah, no," I mumbled but it was too late. My fall was broken by cut grass and manure and I lay face down in cow dung. Smelly, dirty, horrible cow dung. I couldn't let Jill see me like this so I just lay in it and watched her walk past me to her home. What a waste of time. I had spent all day waiting for her and this happened. "Well bollocks to this."

Jill walked down the street to her house. She knocked the front door then went through. When she had shut the door behind her I jumped up and ran towards the west bridge and home. "There is no way I can go home looking like this. My mother will kill me," I hissed.

Two small boys in Darling Street pointed at me and laughed, "Smelly cat! Smelly cat!" at the top of their voices. This only made me more embarrassed and self-conscious and I ran a little bit faster to escape the verbal abuse.

"Thomas, Thomas!" I shouted when I reached the camp. "I fell in cow dung. Can you help me? My mother would skin me if she saw me like this."

Thomas and his buddies all laughed when they saw me.

"You look terrible, Yank," said Matthew.

"Yeah. Come in and we will wash you," said Thomas as he sniggered at my expense.

"What were you doing to get in this state?" asked Paul.

"To tell you the truth I was waiting behind a wall and getting ready to ask Jill out on a date when I fell into the shit."

All the guys laughed some more.

"Don't worry, Yank, you were doing your best. At least you tried," said Thomas. "Now come over and have a shower. You will have to change those clothes too. Matthew, get Yank spare pants and shirt for him."

A few minutes later Matthew came back with olive-green clothes. "Here," he said. "This is standard GI uniform for you. Put them on while your clothes dry. Now you are a real Yank."

When I put the uniform on my heart and chest filled with pride. Today, I'm an American. I felt that I could go and beat Adolf Hitler myself.

A smartly dressed officer approached us. "ATTENTION!" he barked. We all stood still.

"Stand easy," he said, and we all stood down. "Okay, you guys, follow me to that tree. We have a very important visitor arriving shortly. I can't say who it is, just follow me." And with those words we all trooped across the track outside the camp towards the assembly point that our officer wanted us to go to. Reaching the tree, we all sat down and waited for the VIP to appear.

From Castlecoole we watched as a cavalcade of Jeeps and Army vehicles drove down from the building. My stomach turned with excitement. I wondered who this important person was.

A Jeep pulled up alongside us and a man got out. He was the finest dressed soldier I had ever seen. His helmet was polished to perfection. If I was close enough I could see my reflection in his medals too; they gleamed with pride on his chest.

"That's General Patton," said Thomas under his breath.

I was in awe. General George Patton. When I listened to the wireless they always talked about him. My god, what an honour to see this famous man in Enniskillen.

"Attention!" shouted an officer and we all stood in line.

General Patton walked over towards us. "At ease, men. In fact just sit down while I speak to you." We all did as we were told. After all, it is not every day that a three-star general addresses us, especially me. I'm not even a soldier. For a moment he looked straight at me then he looked away and spoke. "No bastard ever won a war by dying for his country. He won a war by letting the other poor bastard die for his!" We all laughed nervously in response. "You men will soon be in action against the some of the toughest fighting troops in the world. Don't underestimate the soldiers of the German Army. We're going to have to kill them and destroy every son-of-a-bitch one of them. Kill them all and use their dead bodies to grease my tank tracks." He took a breath and spoke again. "We Americans are going to win this war and then we will beat those red

Soviet sons of bitches to Berlin. You men don't realise that the war I talk about is almost about to begin. You have been training here in Fermanagh in preparation for the coming attack and let me tell you, it's coming very soon."

His words were tough and meaningful and his powerful message shook me to my very core. War is not fun and games; it's a serious business.

"Okay, men, I will leave you now. I cannot kill any Germans here in Northern Ireland. We will all meet again in France and I will be in my lead tank in Berlin too, and I'm personally going to kill that paperhanging son of a bitch myself."

We all cheered and stood to attention again as Patton got back up on the Jeep. He stood up on the back seat. We saluted him and he saluted back. I could clearly see his white ivory-handled pistols glinting in the warm sun. They then drove off towards Castlecoole where a dinner party was planned for General Patton and his officers.

Arriving back at the camp gates, we were greeted with more excitement.

"Hey, you guys, you'll never guess what has happened. Glen Miller has landed at that RAF airfield up the road. He's going to play with his band at the RUC barracks in Enniskillen tonight.

A big cheer went up.

"That's great news. Where in the town is the RUC barracks and who are the RUC?" said Thomas.

I spoke up. "That's another name for the police station. They are called the Royal Ulster Constabulary or RUC for short."

Thomas looked at me. "Thanks, Yank, for all the information, and you know what? That has given me an idea. We need girls to go so why don't you ask that girl you like to go to the dance? In fact, we will take the Jeep now and go to her house. Knock the front door and ask her out."

My legs turned to jelly. "You are joking, Thomas," I asked.

"No joke," he replied. "Get in and we will see her now."

Reluctantly I got into the Jeep and we drove through the town to her address at the brook. Standing at her front door with Thomas, I shook like crazy. "Stop that. Now don't be stupid, it's only a girl," said Thomas and he then knocked her door. Bang, bang, bang, was the noise the heavy knocker made.

This was the point of no return. My heart skipped a beat.

Thomas looked at me. "Okay, Connor, over to you. I have done all I can. It's your turn now." The door opened and Jill stood there in her cream dress. My heart fluttered in my chest. I felt sickly too.

"Hello," she said. Even the sound of her voice made me quiver. "Can I help you?"

"Y-Y-Yes," I stuttered. "My name is Connor Cleary and I really like you and…" I paused to compose myself and get ready for the bombshell. "I would like to ask you out on a date to see Glen Miller who is playing in the police barracks tonight." I could not believe that I had said that. My head was light with disbelief.

She smiled back at me. "Yes, I'd like to. That's no problem."

I looked at her in astonishment. "You will? That's great! What time can I pick you up?"

She smiled that wonderful smile again. "Nine o'clock would be fine."

"Okay, I will see you then."

Thomas and I got back into the Jeep and drove back to camp.

"Thomas, she said yes," I said in excitement. "I know," said Thomas.

I shook his sleeve. "Thomas, she said yes." "I know," said Thomas.

"But Thomas she said yes!"

"For God's sake calm down, Connor. I know and I'm happy for you."

My thoughts were filled with happiness as we drove through the town. I felt a sense of achievement for the first time. It really wasn't that bad after all, to ask out a girl. My confidence was boosted.

10

The Army trucks poured out of the camp with me on board one of them in a borrowed American uniform that was a few sizes too big. I would be 14 years of age soon so that explained the size problem. Plus, I wouldn't get into a dance until I was 21, so the guys would have to sneak myself and Jill in past the policemen on the gate.

"Where did you say we would meet Jill?" said Thomas.

"Oh, she will be waiting at the top of Darling Street for us," I answered.

"Okay, we will see her there," Thomas replied as our truck rumbled through Enniskillen towards the police barracks.

"June is my favourite month, Thomas. It never really gets dark. It must be almost 9 o'clock and it's still bright."

The sky was clear and a new moon was visible on the lower horizon as we bounced our way in the back of the truck towards Glen Miller and my date with beautiful Jill. When we reached Darling Street I poked my head out of the back of the truck, around its heavy green tarpaulin, and there she stood, shimmering like an angel.

She smiled when she saw me. "Hello, Connor.

Nice to see you again," she said.

"Yes, it's nice to see you too." I reached down with my hand outstretched. "Climb aboard."

She brought her arm up to meet mine and it seemed like it took forever to touch me, like everything had been slowed down. She wore a pretty red dress.

Thomas whistled. "Wow, you look great," he joked. "Yes, I agree too. You look nice."

She blushed and climbed aboard and we revved off across Darling Street and down Queen Street to the RUC Barracks.

On the wall behind the stage hung a Union Jack flag of Great Britain and beside that, the Stars and Stripes of the USA. I took Jill by the hand and we walked into the centre of the dance hall. "Jill, we look to be the only local people here except for the policemen and the other soldiers' dates."

"Yes," she said. "This is going to be fun. I have only heard Glen Miller on our wireless at home. I don't even know what he looks like."

We both stood and faced the stage in anticipation of seeing somebody really famous. The floor was packed with men in uniform and women in wonderful dresses. A man in a smart Army uniform walked onstage to hushed silence. The house lights went off and a spotlight followed him to the middle of the stage. He carried a trombone and his glasses sparkled in the glare of lights.

"Good evening, ladies and gentlemen. It is my honour and pleasure to welcome you all here in Enniskillen Police Barracks this evening. I hope you enjoy our show and music." He turned his back on us and more lights came on, which lit up more band members and fantastic music started to flow from the band and their instruments. In The Mood was the first song they played. We all started dancing straight away. What a great piece of music. We were all still dancing to Little Brown Jug, American Patrol, Don't Sit Under The Apple Tree.

"What a wonderful night. Thanks for asking me to come," said Jill.

"Thanks for coming along and I agree, it has been a great night for me too."

The dancing continued and we swayed slowly, close together, to a sad, slow song called Fools Rush In. The music washed over myself and Jill and poured into my very soul. I would remember this night for a long time.

"Jill, why don't we go for some fresh air? It's very smoky in here," I said.

"Yes, why not? But we can't go out the front door – the policemen there won't let us back in," said Jill.

"Why don't we sneak out the back door then?" So we both crept outside through an open door.

"Look! A boat! Why don't we take it over to Cornagrade and go for a short walk in the fields?"

"Yes, good idea," said Jill.

When we got across to Cornagrade I held her hand. It felt soft and smooth. This is heaven. If I die now I'd die happy, I thought.

It wasn't dark at all for eleven o'clock and the new moon illuminated the fields and countryside for miles around. We both strolled to the top of the hill at Derrygore and stood next to some haystacks. We looked across at Portora School; its prominent stone façade glinted in the moonlight. Moonbeams danced on the ripples of water on the back lough.

"Listen. Do you hear that song that Glen Miller is playing? It's called Blueberry Hill. I will change the words. Let's dance again."

We both started moving to the music coming up from the barracks and I started singing. "I found my thrill on Cornagrade Hill, on Cornagrade Hill when I found you. The moon stood still on Cornagrade Hill and lingered until my dreams came true."

Jill giggled as we slowly danced around the haystacks. I wished this night would never end. I kissed her softly on the cheek and she kissed me on my cheek. My head felt dizzy and light. What a wonderful way to end a wonderful evening. As we walked down Cornagrade Hill we both could hear the sound of our favourite song, Moonlight Serenade, playing in the background.

"That's a lovely tune," said Jill. "Yes, I like it too," I answered.

We both came back across the water to the barracks with the music still sounding its heavenly melody across the town on this calm night.

The very next day, I went to see Thomas in camp.

"Hello, Thomas. That was a great night last night." "Yes, Yank, that is a story to tell your grandkids about when you're an old man."

"Yes, and you will do the same," I said.

He just smiled at me. "Yes, I'm sure I will too once this war is over." All the other guys sat about enjoying the warm sunshine. "We had a tough morning marching with full uniform and kit across the Boho mountains. It was very hot too. The sun was shining down, making it even harder, but ill rest now with the rest of the men."

"Sit down, Yank, and rest yourself," said Paul, but I didn't get the chance to.

"Attention!" said an officer. We all stood up straight.

A car pulled up outside the hut and out stepped General Dwight D. Eisenhower, the allied Army supreme commander. "At ease, men!" he said.

Then General Omar Bradley got out of the green staff car and they both walked towards us. Eisenhower spoke again. "Very soon, men, the invasion of France will begin.

You all will be embarking on a great crusade to free the world of tyranny. Always remember that you are all free Americans and democracy will always prevail." They both walked up to the next hut and said the same thing there.

"That was quick, Thomas. General Patton came and made a great speech. General Eisenhower didn't."

"Yeah, that's the way he operates. No big speeches, just straight to the point," said Thomas.

When they both came back down to the car, General Bradley talked to us. "Men, today I'd like you to play a game of baseball to remind yourself that you are all free Americans and our national game is the world's best pastime."

He got back into the car and the two generals sped off towards the bigger camp at Celtic Park.

"How do you play baseball, Thomas?" I asked.

"You play baseball with a bat and ball, but where are we going to find a baseball diamond around here?" he replied.

"There is a cricket pitch beside Castlecoole. You could play on that," I told him.

It was agreed and we all walked up to the cricket pitch at the hilltop.

"Thomas, you will have to tell me the rules. I have played rounders and my skill at hitting a Hurley ball is excellent."

Thomas looked at me. "Have seen you hitting a Hurley ball. I'm impressed by how far you can send it. That has given me an idea. We could make a few bucks at this today. Leave it to me." He then started to sing, "Take me out to the ball game, take me out on the town. Buy me some peanuts and crackerjacks, I don't care if I never get back, for its one, two, three strikes, and you're out at the old ball game."

We finally made it to the cricket pitch and set about turning it into a baseball diamond.

"Connor, I will tell you the rules and structures as we make the field. There are four bases numbered counter-clockwise: one, two, three, four. There is the infield and the outfield. We will put the bags down for the bases and this, the home base, is simply called home."

The rest of the guys watched Thomas telling me the rules and they rubbed their hands with glee.

"Gee I'm glad Yank is playing with you, Thomas," said Matthew cheerily.

Thomas answered him, "Okay, Matt, put your money where your mouth is. We will play for money."

"Okay, you're on," said Matthew.

We lined out the pitch and in the blazing sun we started to play.

We had been playing all day and I still didn't know the rules. Thomas said we were winning so I took his word for it. Now it was my turn to bat.

"Connor, if you hit this last home run we win the game and the money."

I winked at him. "Don't worry. I'm going to hit it like my Hurley ball. Watch this."

When the pitcher threw the ball at me I batted it over the trees.

Thomas was ecstatic. "YES! What a shot!"

Our team jumped about and hugged each other like little girls. "We won! We won! You are a star!"

I felt so proud of my achievement. This must be what the Captain of an All-Ireland winning Hurling team feels like when he gets the Liam McCarthy into his hands at Croke Park in Dublin. Thomas and I share the money. Lots of coins and notes. It is beautiful to see. Then we all sit down on the cool, fresh grass to relax and drink Coca-Cola as we all sit quiet and reflect on the game. I think I hear bees buzzing in the distance. "Can anyone hear bees?" I ask. We look up at the clear blue sky.

"That's not bees, boys. Look." Above us was the constant drone of aircraft engines and little black dots getting closer. "They are B17 Flying Fortresses in bomber formation."

We all stood up and stared at this amazing sight.

Thousands of aircraft flying east in the big blue sky.

"The invasion must be close, boys. They are not flying to England for the fun of it." Some of the planes were quite low, so low that we could see the pilots and crew in their brown flying jackets. A sombre mood took over us. The war was getting closer for everyone involved.

As the B17s flew on out of sight we all sat back down to rest and think.

It must be sometime later because I dozed off and felt sleepy but I was woken by the sound of another aircraft buzzing low in the sky. "Is that another B17?" I ask wearily.

"Doesn't sound like it." We all jump up.

"Look," I say in astonishment. "That's a Catalina flying boat. What is it doing so far up from Castle Archdale?"

"That plane is in trouble," said Thomas. The flying boat came in sideways, trying to land on the water at Wolf's Lough, but it missed and crashed in the field beside it in a big ball of orange flames. Thick black smoke bellowed upwards into the sky. I stood with the guys in disbelief at what we all had witnessed. I was in shock and wanted to cry.

Once the shock wore off we all started running towards the crash scene. The sound of faraway clanking bells could be heard. It was ambulances, fire engines and police cars driving from Enniskillen to help.

"Quick, boys. Get some buckets of water and we will try and put out this fire."

Everybody stood in a big line starting at the edge of the water and we passed buckets up the line in an attempt to put out the fire.

"I don't think we're going to help anyone now," said Thomas.

"I think they are all dead. It's just too hot to get close to it," said Matthew.

The fire brigade, ambulance and police arrived but it was too late; the crew were all dead.

"How many are aboard?" said Thomas to a passing policeman.

"Eight crew and they are all dead," he answered.

When all the flames were put out the fire brigade and the ambulance men helped remove the bodies from what was left of the black, smouldering wreck. All the bodies smelled like cooked meat; steam was rising from them as they were wrapped in grey blankets and taken away in the ambulance.

"Thomas, from this moment on the war has become real for me."

Thomas nodded his head. "Yes, Connor, and the war has become real for me too."

We both stood and watched the ambulance carrying the dead airmen away to the mortuary.

"I have seen enough for one day, Thomas. I think I will just go home now and see you tomorrow."

"Okay, Connor. I will see you tomorrow."

I left Thomas standing in a daze and I trudged wearily, with my head bowed, home to the cottage.

11

My eyes opened and I looked at the ceiling. "Oh dear. I have slept in!" I exclaimed. It wasn't that I wanted to go to school but I wanted to see if Thomas and his boys were in camp. They were most likely up on the shooting range in the Boho mountains. Everybody else in the house was asleep. Mother and Old Ned sat up most of the night listening to the wireless and the cottage was hushed and still.

"It's nine o'clock. I will put the wireless on."

I got up and turned the little black button with a click. The news was just starting.

"And here is the morning news at nine o'clock from the BBC today, Tuesday 6th of June, 1944," said the announcer in his posh, cut-glass English accent. "Allied forces under the command of General Dwight Eisenhower have landed on the French coast this morning in the Normandy sector at 6am. Heavy fighting has been reported. American, British, Canadian, free French and Polish divisions have all been involved in the military operation to free Europe. The BBC will keep listeners up to date with the fighting as the situation continues."

I turned off the wireless and dressed quickly, then I ran out of my cottage and down to see Thomas. He was standing at the gate on sentry duty. "Thomas, did you hear the news? Your soldiers have landed in France this morning at 6am."

"Yes Connor, I know. They are calling today D-Day. I'm sorry, Connor, but I can't let you on the camp today. It's orders. But I will let you in later if I can."

"That's okay, Thomas. I only came down to tell you the news. I'm taking the day off school to listen to the radio so I will be going back home and sitting by the wireless. Today is going to be one of those days that history will remember for all time and I want to know where I was on that day. Brother Liam can go to hell, the bollocks."

I said goodbye to Thomas and sprinted home to listen to history in the making. All day and all evening Mother Old Ned and I sat in silence listening to the biggest event in our lives. We couldn't even get up to make at cup of tea in case we missed anything that was happening.

"This is the BBC news Tuesday 6th of June 1944. Operation Overlord, D-Day, has been ongoing since 6am. Allied troops have made it ashore and are now building up more forces in a bid to break out across France. Securing the beachhead from counter-attack by German forces has been successful. Men and supplies have been pouring in all day. Prime Minister Winston Churchill has congratulated everybody involved. The beach code names for sectors were Gold, Sword, Juno, Omaha and Utah. American forces took heavy casualties at Omaha but fought the Germans until they prevailed."

At the end of 6th of June 1944, I was exhausted. I think it is bedtime.

It had been a momentous day in history and I would never forget where I was on that day. I was tired. I put my head down on my pillow to sleep but my thoughts were with all those brave soldiers because for some of them, today, 6th of June, was their last day to be alive on Earth.

Thomas must face all that fighting very soon. I fell asleep feeling sad and depressed.

12

Brother Liam stood in the classroom in front of us. He was still a complete bastard and today was the day when I wouldn't put up with this any longer. If he picks on me he is going to be sorry.

"Rodgers!" he bellowed. "Get up here now, boy."

Jimmy walked up to the front of the class and Brother Liam thumped him with his fist.

"Now sit down."

He took out his cane and made him put out his hand. "I'll cut the hands off you, boy," and he did. His hands were red raw. Then he stared at me. This is it, I thought. "Connor Cleary, or Yank as you have been called. Get up here, now."

"No, sir, I won't," I said. "WHAT?" he replied.

"No, sir, you heard me the first time."

The whole class sat in stunned silence and Brother Liam's face went beetroot red. I thought it would explode. He made a run for me from the top of the class. This was my only chance of getting away. As he got close to me I jumped up and kicked the cunt full in the balls and he went down like all bullies do, very fast.

A cheer went up around the classroom but I was not waiting for him to get up because he would kill me for sure, so I opened the window and jumped out. My knee hit the bottom window sill. "God, that's sore!" I shouted, but at least I had escaped.

I will never go back to school again. I need a job. I will go to the railway station and see if they need a boy to start. They always do.

A man stood at the platform in a uniform and smart peaked cap. "Excuse me, sir, is there any work going here?"

The man looked at me. "What is your name, son?" he said.

"Connor Cleary," I said.

"Is your mother Kathleen out in the cottage?" "YES, and Old Ned too," I answered.

"I know your family. Well, we have a job going as a porter. Can you start tomorrow?"

I was delighted. "Yes, I can."

"Alright, be back at the railway station at 9am tomorrow. See you then."

I ran off down the street. "I have a job! I will tell Thomas. He will be happy."

When I got to the Dublin road the police had blocked it. "What is happening?"

"The Americans are leaving. You can't go down that way," said a policeman.

I knew a shortcut so I ran through the trees trying to see Thomas. My heart was pounding with fear and excitement. When I reached the camp I could only get to the barbwire fence. Thomas was putting things onto a truck. "Thomas!" I shouted. "Thomas!"

He looked across and saw me and smiled. "Give me a minute and I will be over to you." He filled the truck and came across to me. We both stood facing each other at the fence. "Hello, Yank. I mean, Connor Cleary. We have to go now. We're taking the trucks and going straight to Belfast by road. Ships are waiting to take us to France. We will be in the War very soon."

I wiped tears from my eyes. "Thomas Schulman, you have been my best friend in the whole world. I'm going to miss you. Please stay safe and listen to what Old Ned said. Keep your head down and you'll get through it."

Thomas put his hand in his pocket and took out a baseball. "Here, take this. It was found at Ebbets Field, home of my team, the Brooklyn Dodgers. Have you still got the pebble, Connor?"

I wiped more tears. "Yes, Thomas, I still have the pebble that you give me and here is something else for you." I took my Hurley ball out and gave it to him. We both swapped our sports balls through the wire fence.

"Connor, I have your Hurley ball and the pebble you gave me that day we went on the Jeep. I will keep them always and think of you. Now I must leave you." We both shook hands. "Connor, I will see you soon."

"Yes, Thomas. I will see you soon. I will write to you also."

Thomas turned away and walked to the big green truck. He got into the back and the soldiers thundered out of the camp and sped off to Belfast to the waiting ships.

***

"Sixty years have flown by, Thomas, and the last time I spoke to you I was crying my eyes out like a baby. Today I'm an old man and I'm still crying. This is the first time I have been so close to you since that day at the barbwire fence in Enniskillen in 1944, when you give me your baseball and I gave you my Hurley ball. I have the pebble with me too. I just hope you have both items in your pocket with you now, but sadly you can't speak to me."

The Star of David headstone was easy to find in a sea of crosses in the American military Cemetery and now I can read the name on it. Private First Class Thomas Schulman, 8th Infantry Division, United States Army, 1st of March 1926, 26th of July 1944. More tears flow down my face.

"Thomas, why did you have to die? You never got a chance to have a proper life. You were cut down so young, like all of the boys buried here with you. Did your family in New York miss you? You never got the chance to see them again, or marry Lola and have children.

"Enniskillen has changed since you were there. Our cottage, Old Ned, my mother and the railway line have all gone. It's only me left alive. Why did it have to be you, Thomas, that had to get killed here in France so far away from your home in New York?

"You made me the person that I became with your friendly smile and your words of worldly wisdom. The few short months you were in Enniskillen had to be the best time of my life. Every day I live I always think back to 1943 and 1944 as the best time of my life. My favourite music will always be Glen Miller and Frank Sinatra. Rita Hayworth and Betty Grable will always be my favourite girls. Laurel and Hardy and the Marx Brothers are my favourite comedians for all time and everything positive that happened in my life is all down to you, Thomas. So I have come here today to thank you. Here is the pebble that you gave me in 1943. I believe it is Jewish custom to leave a stone at the grave of a friend or loved one."

I took the pebble from my pocket and placed next to the little American flag by Thomas's headstone.

"Goodbye for now, Thomas. I know I'll see you someday soon."

I stood to attention and saluted in the US Army style.

"I might be an old man now, Thomas, but at heart I'm still and will always be Connor Cleary. A BOY CALLED YANK."